This book is number 785 of a strictly limited edition of 1,000 copies.

With good wishes,

Warwick Coll

The Sonnets